Presented To

_____

From

_____

Date

_____

BETHANY BACKYARD®
www.bethanyhouse.com

Published by Bethany House Publishers
11400 Hampshire Avenue South
Bloomington, Minnesota 55438
www.bethanyhouse.com

Bethany House Publishers is a Division of
Baker Book House Company, Grand Rapids, Michigan.

Printed in the United States of America

Library of Congress Cataloging-in-Publication data applied for.

ISBN 0-7642-2750-5

Dear Grown-up,

The young child's response to Christmas is up close and personal. And something happens for us when we look at the coming of Christ into the world through a young child's imaginative eyes: Our own faith is freshened.

That's why the Scripture verses are included in this book— for your own meditation. For example, in one prayer-poem the child asks *when* Christmas is coming. And the accompanying verse (1 Peter 1:20) reminds us, as adults, that Christ's coming was part of God's plan before the creation of the world. Yet people of faith waited centuries for the promise to be fulfilled. Our waiting for Christmas is a symbol of their expectation.

So share this book and Advent with your young child. And may God richly bless you both!

Elspeth Campbell Murphy

Is it Christmas yet, God?

Christ was chosen before the world was made. But he was shown to the world in these last times for you.

1 PETER 1:20

Christmas is coming I know—
But *when*?
When the tree is up,
Is it Christmas then?
Is it Christmas when presents
Are piled up high?
Or when stars go dancing?
And angels fly?

Christmas comes, I'll

But *how*?
Is it Christmas yet, God?
Is it now?
Now?
NOW?

Christmas Lights

The people who walked in darkness have seen a great light. They lived in a land of shadows, but now light is shining on them.

ISAIAH 9:2 (TEV)

It's past my bedtime,
But out I go.
Out in the dark
   And cold
   And snow.
Out in this darkest
Of wintry nights.
Out in the dark—
To see the *lights*!

Nativity

Today your Savior was born in David's town. He is Christ, the Lord. This is how you will know him: You will find a baby wrapped in cloths and lying in a feeding box.

LUKE 2:11–12

Angels and donkeys,
Shh!
Gather round.
Wise Men and camels,
Shh!
Don't make a sound.
Silently, shepherds,
Come with your sheep.
Shh!
Softly, so softly . . .

The Baby's asleep.

Christmas Pageant

Who can this little
shepherd boy be?
Look closer, God.
Ta-Daa!
It's ME!

The shepherds said to each other,
"Let us go to Bethlehem and see
this thing that has happened. We
will see this thing the Lord told us
about."

LUKE 2:15

Treetop Angel

Look at me, God!
I'm way up high!
I feel like an angel
In the sky!

I'm putting the angel
On top of our tree.
And the angel is waiting
Just like me

For Christmas
For Christmas
For Christmas to come!

Follow the Star

[The wise men] saw the same star they had seen in the east. It went before them until it stopped above the place where the child was. When the wise men saw the star, they were filled with joy.

MATTHEW 2:9b–10

Come with me, Wise Men.
We'll follow the star.
We'll ride on our camels
   A long time
   And far.
We will go on a journey
And look to the sky.
We will search for the Baby,
The Wise Men and I.

Glitter!

Mercy, peace and love be yours

in abundance.

Glitter on Grandma's
   Christmas card,
Glitter on the floor,
Glitter on my chair,
And just outside the door—
Glittery little snowflakes
Are falling on the tree.
Glitter, glitter everywhere!
Especially on me!

Toys

God loves the person who gives *happily.*

2 CORINTHIANS 9:7b

You know what, God?
Some kids have a lot of stuff.
Other kids don't have enough.
That's why a kid
I'll never see
Will get a Christmas gift—
From me!

It's a Secret

Everything good comes from God, and every perfect gift is from him.

JAMES 1:17a

God,
How do you keep a secret in
When it wants to pop out?
How do you make a secret hush
When it wants to shout?
How do you hold a secret down
When it wants to play?
Oh, *how* do you make a secret *wait*
Until . . .
Christmas . . .
DAY?

Along the Road to Bethlehem

At that time, Augustus Caesar sent an order to all people in the countries that were under Roman rule. The order said that they must list their names in a register. . . . And everyone went to their own towns to be registered. So Joseph left Nazareth, a town in Galilee. He went to the town of Bethlehem in Judea. The town was known as the town of David. Joseph went there because he was from the family of David.

LUKE 2:1, 3–4

Along the road to Bethlehem,
Oh, Mary!
Let me go with you.
And when your little boy is born,
Oh, Mary!
Let me be there, too.
I'll hold the baby.
(I know how.)
Oh, Mary!
Take me with you now.
I'll sing my favorite lullaby
And rock him if he starts to cry.
And you'll be glad
I'm there, you'll see.
Oh, Mary!
Mary! Wait
For me.

Little Donkey

While Joseph and Mary were in
Bethlehem, the time came for her
to have the baby.

LUKE 2:6

Little donkey
Sweet and shy,
I know where you're going,
Clopping by.

Clopping by
While angels soar—
You'll carry His mother
To the stable door.

Swaddling Clothes

She gave birth to her first son.
There were no rooms left in the
inn. So she wrapped the baby
with cloths and laid him in a
box where animals are fed.

LUKE 2:7

Tiny baby,
newly born,
we'll wrap you up
to keep you warm,
to keep you snug
and safe from harm.
Oh, tiny Jesus!
Newly born.

Christmas Eve

Later, Jesus talked to the people again. He said, "I am the light of the world. The person who follows me will never live in darkness. He will have the light that gives life."

JOHN 8:12

Guess what, God!
If I
Sit very still,
And
Hold on to it tight,
Then I
Get to have
My own CANDLE tonight!

Christmas Day

This is the day that the Lord
has made. Let us rejoice and be
glad today!

PSALM 118:24

You know what, God?
I waited
And waited
For Christmas Day.
But it always seemed
So far away.

Then this morning,
When I opened my eyes,
Christmas
Jumped up
And yelled,
"SURPRISE!"

Merry Christmas, God!

For unto us a child is born, unto us a son is given: and the government shall be upon his shoulder: and his name shall be called Wonderful, Counsellor, The mighty God, The everlasting Father, The Prince of Peace.

ISAIAH 9:6 (KJV)